What Happens Next?

by Sandra Markle

For Maris Mann,
whose friendship supports me
no matter what happens

Published by
LONGSTREET PRESS, INC.
A subsidiary of Cox Newspapers,
A division of Cox Enterprises, Inc.
2140 Newmarket Parkway
Suite 118
Marietta, GA 30067

Printed in the United States of America
1st printing 1995
ISBN 1-56352-232-2

Jacket and book design by Jill Dible
Electronic film prep and separations by Advertising Technologies Inc., Atlanta, GA

The author would like to express special thanks to Dr. Charles Barman, professor of science and environmental education, Indiana University, and Dr. James Barufaldi, professor of science education and director of the Science Education Center at the University of Texas at Austin, for sharing their expertise and enthusiasm.

What Happens Next?

Reader's Note: To help readers pronounce words that may not be familiar to them, a pronunciation guide appears on page 34. These words are italicized the first time they appear in the text.

Did you think the squirrel on the book's cover would fall to the ground? Now, you can see it's a flying squirrel with folds of skin that stretch out to catch the wind. But it's gliding too fast to land safely. What do you think the squirrel will do to slow down?

You'll need to tackle this puzzle—and all the puzzles in this book—in two steps. First, look at the picture for clues. For example, does the squirrel have any special features it could use to slow down? Then *brainstorm*. Think of all the things that could happen next—good or bad. When you think you know, turn the page.

Did you figure out that the squirrel transforms its body from *glider* to *parachute*? At just the right instant, the flying squirrel stretches out its front feet, digging its claws into the tree trunk. Touchdown!

Can you design a glider that catches air to fly the way a flying squirrel does? First, collect materials you can find around the house that you could use to build a glider. You might want to use straws and paper or a styrofoam plate. Next, brainstorm, thinking about how the squirrel flies. Draw a diagram of your glider. Think how you might improve it. Finally, build and test your glider. How far does it glide? Make any changes you think will make it glide farther.

Here are plans for one glider to start your creative juices flowing.

1. Use **scissors** to cut a **sheet of plain paper** into a square. Fold the square in half. Unfold it.
2. Fold the two top corners into the center.
3. Fold the tip of the triangle down to the bottom edge.
4. Fold the two top corners into the center.
5. Fold the triangle in half. Turn it upside down so the base is on top. The point has three layers. The middle layer is the glider's body. Lift the other two, forming wings. Cut off the middle layer's point about five centimeters up from the tip.

Tape the tail together and slide a **paper clip** onto the nose fold. Now you have a glider. Toss it forward. Like the squirrel kicking off, this toss powers the flight. Fast-flowing air moving away from the glider sucks the wings up. Slower-moving air below the wings pushes up. *Gravity*, the force that tugs everything toward the earth, slows the glider as it moves through the air. When it slows so much that there's not enough lift to support it, the flight ends.

Materials you need to do any activity are shown in bold type so you can easily see what to collect before you start.

4

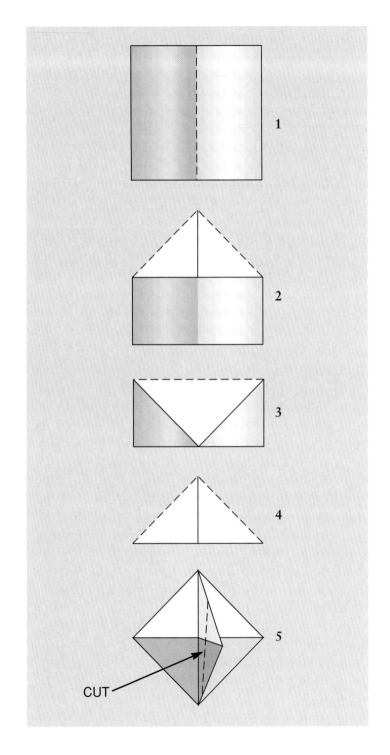

A lizard soaks up most of the heat energy it needs to be active from the air and ground. But even a lizard can get too hot. This lizard needs some way to escape the heat, but it lives in a *desert* in Africa where there isn't much water or shade. What is it likely to do next?

Things you learned in the past can help you solve puzzles. Have you ever hopped from one bare foot to another on a hot beach or sidewalk to cool off? Then you're probably not surprised to see the lizard lifting as much of its body as possible off the sand. This reduces the amount of heat the lizard soaks up. The lizard also hops back and forth from one set of feet to the other. You could say it dances to beat the heat.

One way your body cools off when it starts to overheat is by producing *sweat*—the liquid that pours out onto your skin. Why does sweating help? Try this experiment to find out.

On a warm, sunny day, put **clean cotton tube socks** on like mittens. Wet one and go outdoors. Hold your hands up and count to twenty. Which hand feels cooler—the wet one or the dry one?

The wet one should feel cooler. As the water in the wet sock heats up, it *evaporates*, or changes to *water vapor*, a gas, and moves into the air. Some of the heat energy needed for this to happen comes from your body. And when you lose heat you feel cooler. Now imagine how you'd feel if sweat were evaporating from all over your body.

What do you think happened before this polar bear sprawled on the snow? It may help you to know that a bear's hair is nearly as see-through as plastic wrap, letting the sun's heat energy easily reach its skin. And a polar bear's skin is black—the best color for soaking up this heat energy. When the bear is active, its body also gives of some heat which is trapped by all that thick fur. Did you figure out that the polar bear stretched out on the snow when it got too warm? How will this cool off the bear? *Clue*: Think about how the lizard warms up.

Will this olive oil form a layer under the water? Will it float on the surface? Or will it *dissolve*, breaking up into tiny droplets suspended in the water?

You may have never seen what happens when any kind of oil is added to water. So you will probably need more information to *predict* what will happen here. How can you solve this puzzle?

You could ask someone who knows, but the best way is to see for yourself. So pour a tablespoon of **olive oil** into a **glass of water**. Stir five times to mix. Then look closely. Although the oil looks heavier than water, it is really much lighter and so it floats.

Now, test each of the following materials to see how it reacts with water: **salt**, **vinegar**, **milk** (chocolate or plain), **vegetable oil**, and **sugar**. Wash out the **glass** with **soap** and water between each test.

Copy this chart and make an X to show what happens.

Repeat each test to be sure what you discovered will happen more than once. Even better, retest a third time, the way scientists do.

TESTED	DISSOLVES	SINKS	FLOATS
Olive oil			
Salt			
Vinegar			
Milk			
Vegetable oil			
Sugar			

Now, float oil-based hobby paint on water to make something special.

Set an **aluminum pie pan** half full of **water** on **newspaper**. Use **scissors** to cut **plain white paper** into fourths. Drip several drops of two or three different colors of **oil-based hobby paint** (used to paint models) onto the water. Drag a small, **plastic comb** through the drops, creating swirls. Place the paper on top of the paint. Count to three, lift, and lay—clean side down—on newspaper to dry.

You may use this paper as a book mark. How else could you use it?

This activity can be messy, so get an adult's permission or work with an adult partner. Wear old clothes and clean up when finished. Remove any paint from fingers with fingernail polish remover.

This *tanker* ship is on fire and leaking oil. Is it likely to cause more trouble for birds that land on the water or for fish swimming in the depths? How do you know?

If the waves move the oil toward the beach, what do you think will happen next?

See the tiny piece of wood the wasp is removing from the board with its hard, beak-like mouth parts? What will the wasp do with the wood? To help you find out, think about what people make from wood. Then decide which of these things the wasp might be able to make. When you think you know what happens next, turn the page.

Did you guess that the wasp would make paper and use it to build a nest? This wasp's nest was built by a different type of wasp than the one you saw collecting wood, but they both use the same paper-making process. After the wasps abandoned the nest at the end of the summer, it was cut open so you can peek inside. The paper cells were where baby wasps developed. The outside layers protected the wasps from wind and rain.

A special tool called a *scanning electron microscope* was used to enable you to take a close look at wasp paper and man-made typing paper. In what ways do the papers look alike? How are they different?

To make paper, the wasp chews the wood, mixing it with water it drank and stored inside its body. Once a paste forms, the wasp presses it into a ball and carries it home. Then the wasp chews the ball to soften it and spreads out a thin layer of paper. Slowly—layer upon layer—the nest takes shape. The queen wasp builds the first few cells. Then her offspring add onto the nest while she stays home, laying eggs. As the number of offspring grows, so does the nest.

Man-made typing paper

Wasp paper

This activity can be messy, so get an adult's permission or work with an adult partner. Wear old clothes and clean up when finished.

Follow the directions to make your own paper. How many ways can you think of to use this paper?

Tear **20 sheets of newspaper** into tiny pieces. Soak in a **bowl** of **water** overnight. Cover your work area with **newspapers** and a stack of three **paper towels.** Have an adult cut a **13 centimeter square of window screen** (available at hardware stores). Use **scissors** to cut **waxed paper** squares the same size.

Pour two cups of water into a **blender.** Add a cup of wet paper and a **tablespoon of cornstarch.** Blend until it looks like a gray milkshake. Pour into a **clean bowl.** Push the screen into the bowl until it's covered with mush and lift straight up. Top with waxed paper. Flip, waxed paper side down, onto the towels. Cover with three more paper towels. Use a **rolling pin** to squeeze out water. Remove the wet towels and screen. Turn over onto a dry paper towel, peel off the waxed paper and let dry. Repeat to make more paper.

What team work! These weaver ants of Australia have pulled the edges of the leaf together. If they can make the edges stay together, they can use the curled leaf as a nest. But how can they do that? Look around. Make a list of everything you find that is used to hold things together. Looking at how similar puzzles have been solved can help you think of a solution. What do you think the ants will do to hold the leaf edges together?

LARVA

Now, you can see that the ants are using sticky threads. Wondering where these sticky threads come from? They're made by an ant *larva*, or young ant. The ant larva produces silk threads to spin a case around itself before it changes into an adult. When the worker holds the larva against the leaf and squeezes, a drop of *silk* comes out. Then the worker moves the larva, pulling the silk into a sticky thread.

Here are two *glues* you can test. Put the white of an **egg** in one **tea cup** and whip with a **fork**. In the other **cup**, blend 1/4 cup **flour** and 4 tablespoons **water**. Use **scissors** to cut two identical strips of **typing paper**. Spread egg glue on half of one strip, fold over the unglued half, and press. Repeat with the flour glue. After an hour, check: Which glue is still stuck? Which stays stuck when you try to pull the paper apart? Can you think of anything else that might make a better glue? Check with an adult to be sure it's safe to test.

Use the glue that worked best to stick a picture you colored to poster board. When it's dry, cut into eight irregularly shaped pieces, creating a puzzle. Share with a friend.

When the female giant water bug lays her eggs, she produces a glue and sticks them to the male's back. The eggs need care, but her front legs are too short for her to reach her own back. For one thing, the eggs need water pushed over them so the developing young get a steady supply of oxygen from the water.

Why else do you think it helps the baby bugs to stick with a parent? Once the young hatch, the glue washes off and the empty eggs drop off the male's back.

At the sight of mom arriving with dinner, this blue heron chick rushed to get fed. But it lost its balance. Now, the baby bird is struggling to keep from falling. What will happen next? Brainstorm. Make a list of at least five different things you think could happen. Then decide which is the most likely to happen. You should know this bird's nesting tree is in a swamp.

This was too bad for the bird, but lucky for the hungry alligator. Both the bird and alligator are part of a *food chain*. *Green plants*, like those making the water look green, are the beginning of every food chain. They make and store food as sugars and starches. In this food chain, insects eat the plants. Fish eat the insects. Then the mother heron catches fish for her babies. The last link in the food chain, so far, is the alligator.

You may be surprised to learn that you're part of a food chain, too. For example, the milk you drink comes from a cow that eats green grass. When you eat a green plant, your energy comes directly from the source. So grow your own green plants for a tasty snack.

Soak a **paper towel** in water and squeeze out the excess. Fold this into fourths and sprinkle on **alfalfa seeds** (available at health-food stores and plant nurseries). Slide the damp paper and seeds into a **quart-size, self-sealing plastic bag,** but don't seal. Place in a warm, shady place.

The alfalfa seeds will sprout in a few days. When the stems are about eight centimeters long, rinse and tuck into half a **pita bread.** Add **cheese, tomato**—anything you like. Top with a teaspoon of your favorite **salad dressing.** Enjoy!

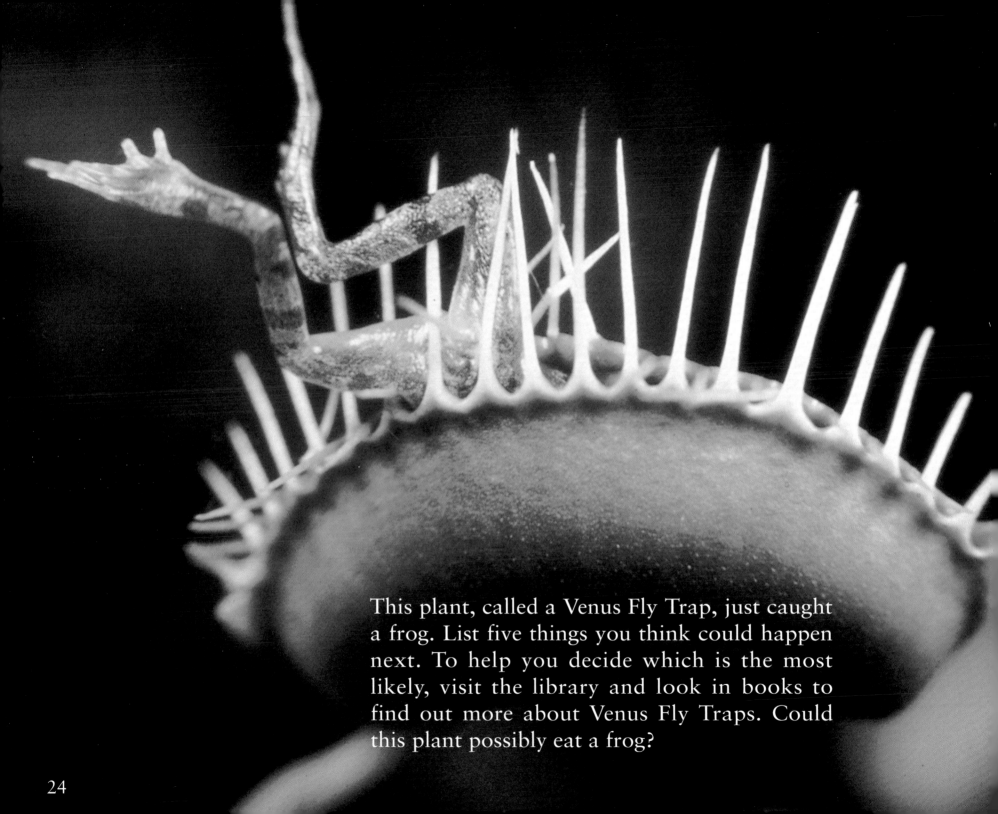

This plant, called a Venus Fly Trap, just caught a frog. List five things you think could happen next. To help you decide which is the most likely, visit the library and look in books to find out more about Venus Fly Traps. Could this plant possibly eat a frog?

See the fuzzy *fungi* growing on this jack o'lantern? Fungi are plants, but they're usually not green. That's because they don't make their own food. They get what they need to grow by using an animal or another plant for food. What will happen to the jack o'lantern as the fungi continue to grow? It would help to take a closer look at the fungi and find out where they get the food they need to grow. You'll find this information on the next page.

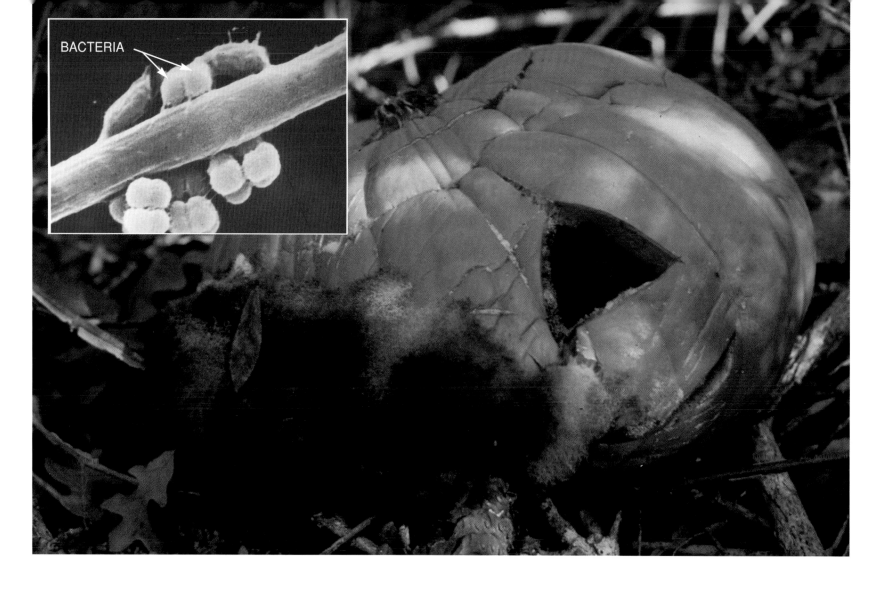

BACTERIA

Here you can see one of the many thread-like strands that the fungi spread through the jack o'lantern. What look like spots are *bacteria*, living things that grow with the fungi. These give off special juices that make any part of the jack o'lantern they touch *decompose* or break down, forming a liquid food.

Now, use what you learned to decide what will happen as the fungi continue to grow.

Did you guess that the jack o'lantern would break down until only the tough outer skin and stem were left?

You may be surprised to learn that when the food supplied by the jack o'lantern is used up and the fungi die, the bacteria uses it for food. The bacteria produces even more food than it can use. But this extra food isn't wasted. It soaks into the ground and spreads through the soil. Some of this food material provides the minerals that green plants need to grow and make food. And that starts new food chains.

Are there some things that fungi and bacteria, nature's clean-up team, won't decompose? This activity will help you find out.

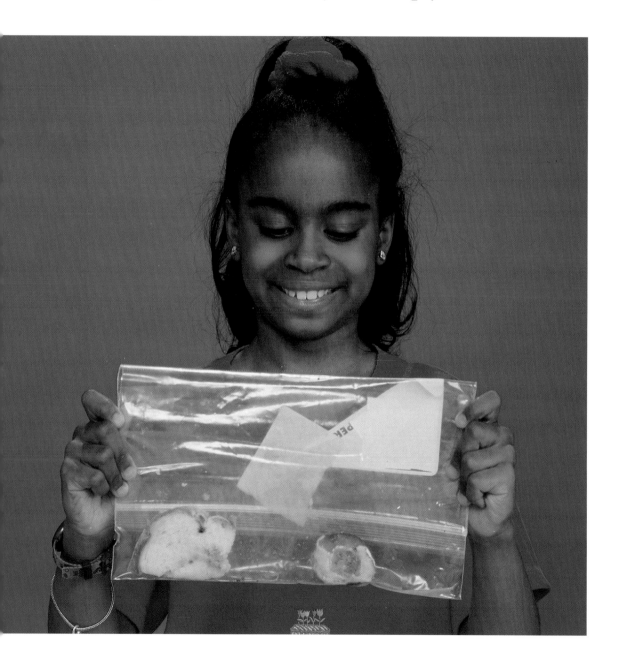

Put a slice of **potato**, a **metal paper clip**, a **scrap of paper**, and **1/4 of a slice of bread** in a **quart-sized self-sealing plastic bag**. Sprinkle with **water** and seal. Place the bag inside a warm cupboard. After a few days, start checking for fuzzy fungi. It might be white or colored because there are different kinds of fungi.

Which items did the fungi decompose? What do these have in common? Go on a walk outdoors with an adult partner. Can you find fungi in action? Point out things fungi could decompose and things it could not decompose.

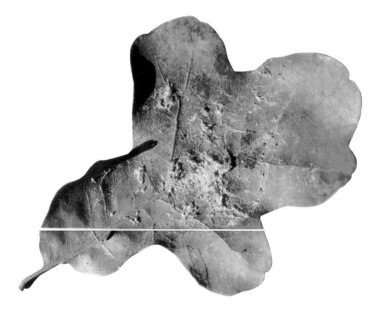

Every fall, many of the trees in the forest drop their leaves. So if you go for a walk, will you sink up to your eyeballs in dead leaves? Perhaps the leaf with fungi growing on it is a clue that could help you solve this puzzle.

What if you were playing on the beach and looked up to see these clouds? What would you do next? Now you know how to solve puzzles—look for clues and brainstorm to think of all the things that could happen next. It can help to remember past experiences, so think if you've ever seen clouds like these before.

Predicting what will happen next can help you discover fascinating things going on all around you. It can even help you make choices that will keep you safe.

THINGS TO DO

These activities will give you more chances to predict what will happen next. Then keep on investigating to find out what does happen.

❀ Start a mini-garden in **flower pots** or even sturdy **styrofoam cups** that have a hole poked in the bottom to let water drain out. Fill each pot or cup almost full with **potting soil** (available at gardening centers). Buy packages of **flower or vegetable seeds**. Plant three to four seeds per pot, pushing each seed just beneath the surface. Sprinkle with **water** every other day and cover with **plastic wrap** until the sprouts first appear. Then try these tests.

• Set two or three pots in a sunny place and the same number inside a dark cupboard. Watch for the seedlings to get their first leaves. Then predict which will grow longer stems— the ones in the sunlight or the ones in the dark.

• Plant six pots of seeds. When they sprout, water three pots with plain water and three with **fertilizer**. (An adult can help you measure the correct amount of fertilizer into the water.) Predict which will grow taller and measure the plants as they grow. Also predict which will grow more leaves and count to check yourself.

❀ The next time it's summer, look for caterpillars on plants. When you find one, ask an adult partner to wear gloves and gently move the caterpillar to a quart jar. Add a sturdy twig for climbing and lots of the leaves like those the caterpillar was eating. Caterpillars need to eat a lot as they develop, and many eat only one or two types of plants. Cover the jar with plastic wrap secured with a rubber band. Punch lots of holes in the plastic with a sharp pencil to let in fresh air. Watch the caterpillars, predict what will happen next, and keep on watching. When, after a stage called a pupa, a mature butterfly or moth emerges, take it back where you found the caterpillar and set it free.

Pronunciation Guide

BACTERIA	bak´ tirē ə
DECOMPOSE	dēkəm, ´pōz
DISSOLVE	də̇´zlälv
ELECTRON	ə̇´lek, trän
EVAPORATE	ə̇´vapə, rāt
FUNGI	fən, jī
GLIDER	glīdə(r)
GRAVITY	`gravəd · ē
LARVA	`lärvə
MICROSCOPE	`mīkrə, skōp
PARACHUTE	`parə, shüt
SILK	`silk
SWEAT	`swet

ä as in cart   ə as in banana   ü as in rule

34

Glossary and Index

BACTERIA: Tiny living things. Some types break down plant and animal matter, producing a liquid. What they don't use may pass into the soil, supplying green plants with some of the minerals needed to grow and produce food. (Singular: bacterium) **26-29**

BRAINSTORM: To come up with a list of possible solutions to a puzzle or problem. **1, 21, 30**

DECOMPOSE: To break down living material into smaller bits that are then recycled in the environment. **26-28**

DESERT: Any place that is very dry. The desert pictured in this book is the Namibian Desert in Africa. **5**

DISSOLVE: To have something break down into such small particles that each is completely surrounded by a liquid. For example, when sugar is stirred into water and seems to disappear, it has dissolved. **9-10**

EVAPORATE: The process through which a liquid changes to a gas. For example, when rainwater in a puddle is warmed by the sun's heat energy, it changes into water vapor, a gas, and moves into the air. **7**

FOOD CHAIN: A sequence in which food energy is moved from green plants to animals. Green plants produce and store food, then animals eat the plants, and these animals may be eaten by other animals. For example, a caterpillar eats a green leaf, a bird eats the caterpillar, and then a snake eats the bird. **22-27**

FUNGI: Special kinds of living things that are not capable of producing food for themselves. Some types help break down plant and animal matter. (Singular: fungus) **25-29**

GLIDER: Anything without an engine that is carried along by the wind. **2-4**

GLUE: Any sticky material used to bond things together. For centuries, people have made glue from animal bones, corn, potatoes, and natural rubber. Today, most glues are made of special chemicals—some are even strong enough to stick parts of cars and airplanes together. **18-20**

GRAVITY: Force that pulls things to the ground. **4**

GREEN PLANTS: Plants that appear green in color because they contain a special chemical called chlorophyll. When chlorophyll is present, plants are able to capture sunlight and use it to produce food in the form of sugar. **22-24, 27, 32-33**

LARVA: The young, immature form of an animal. Some, like ants and butterflies, look completely different from the adults. Others just look like smaller versions of the adults. (Plural: larvae) **18**

PARACHUTE: Anything umbrella shaped. When expanded it slows the speed of something moving through the air. **2**

PREDICT: Make a carefully thought-out guess based on past experiences and what's been observed. **9, 30, 32**

SCANNING ELECTRON MICROSCOPE: A special tool capable of magnifying objects up to 300,000 times—enough to see inside cells. **15**

SILK: Special material produced by certain insects and spiders. It begins as a liquid, flows out through tiny tubes and openings, and is pulled to make it change into a solid thread. **18**

SWEAT: Liquid, also called perspiration, produced by special groups of cells in the skin and poured out onto the surface to help cool off the body when it gets too warm. **7**

TANKER: A ship with large tanks for carrying oil. **12**

WATER VAPOR: Water in the form of a gas. **7**